P9-CCR-806

Adam Smith Goes to School

Bernard Wolf

J. B. Lippincott Company/Philadelphia and New York

For Lois Young, who has not forgotten
that learning can be adventure.

The author wishes to express his gratitude to the following persons for their generous assistance and support during the preparation of this book: Dorothy Briley, Jean Krulis, and Carlos Crosbie of J. B. Lippincott Company; Stanley Seidman, principal, Hunter Elementary School, New York City, for his enthusiasm and trust; Patricia Mansur, Joseph Kubat, and Leonard Schoenfeld, teachers at Hunter Elementary School, and all the wonderful children in Mrs. Young's class there; and Mike Levins, who, with his usual darkroom wizardry, produced the photographic prints for this book. And last but certainly not least, many, many thanks to a likeable young fellow whose name really is Adam Smith!

Printed in the United States of America
2 4 6 8 9 7 5 3 1

U.S. Library of Congress Cataloging in Publication Data. Wolf, Bernard. Adam Smith goes to school. SUMMARY: A photographic essay depicting a six-year-old boy's experiences during his first week in school. [1. School stories] I. Title. PZ7.W81858Ad [E] 77-17269
ISBN-O-397-31764-6

This is an important day for Adam Smith.
Today is his first day of school.

"I am your teacher, Mrs. Young. We have a lot to learn together this year. Now, when I strike this chime, everyone must stop what he or she is doing and gather around me in a large circle."

“I have name tags for each of you to wear today. They will make getting to know one another easier.”

Each first-grade student is given a special place to put his or her lunch box and personal belongings.

When all her students have put away their things, Mrs. Young asks them to sit around her in a circle again. "For our first lesson, I will read you a story," she says.

Reading looks *easy* when Mrs. Young does it. But Adam isn't so sure that it is as easy as it looks.

Mrs. Young asks Adam to read aloud to her. "A very good beginning, Adam," she tells him. "Now I know where to start you in your reading workbook."

While Mrs. Young tests the reading skills of other students, Adam and a new friend work with a board game that teaches them how to use a ruler for measuring.

"This is your math workbook," says Mrs. Young. "Try the first two pages and let me see how well you do."

At first Adam needs a little help from his friend Jeffrey.

17
18
19
20

Soon he is able to work on his own. Before he knows it, it is time for lunch and swapping funny stories. "What did one toe say to the other?" asks Adam. "'Don't look now, but there's a heel following us!'"

The Hundreds Board makes learning to count from one to one hundred fun. You draw the numbers one by one from the bowl and find the right places for them on the board.

The bell signaling the end of the school day will ring soon.

Everybody's a little tired, including Mrs. Young.

Bright and early the next day, Mrs. Young has something new to show the class. They will learn to use the metric system to measure things. She is holding a cube that is exactly one cubic centimeter in size.

"The plus sign is used to show that you are adding to a number," Mrs. Young tells the class. "One plus five equals six, and we have a special sign that means 'equals.' And, the answer to an addition problem is called a sum."

Today Gillian needs a little help from Adam with her math workbook.

SIX MILLION
DOLLAR MAN

Once a week the class goes to the music room, where Mrs. Mansur teaches a music appreciation class.

Today Mrs. Mansur puts on a recording of circus music. She asks the children to pretend they are working in a circus. Each can choose what he or she wants to be — a clown, an elephant, a giraffe, a tiger.

The music begins. There seem to be three clowns.

And everybody gets into the act.

"I understand that a few somebodies were pretty noisy in Mrs. Mansur's class!" scolds Mrs. Young. "We won't mention any names today, since I'm certain that it won't happen again."

MILK

The first lesson the following day is science. Mrs. Young shows the children how to put a sweet potato in water so they can watch it grow roots and sprout leaves.

Each student is taught to use the record player in the listening corner. There are recordings of books being read.

By listening to the record and following along in the book, the students improve their reading skills.

Adam and a classmate work in the block corner until it is time to go to their physical education class.

“Everybody stretch! As high as you can!”

The “snake” exercise turns into friendly rough and tumble.

NY

Later that afternoon there's more serious work to be done. By matching colored strips to places in their math workbooks, the students get a better understanding of metric measurement.

Mrs. Young explains a lesson in the reading workbook. The students must match the pictures up correctly with the sentences.

1
her mother are at the store.
getting some food
you to eat.
of a good surprise
make a cake for her dad.

Everybody makes a bookmark with his or her name on it to use with the reading workbooks.

Lunchtime is special today. It is Elizabeth's sixth birthday, and her mother has sent cupcakes to school so the class can help her celebrate.

After the birthday party, the class goes to Mr. Schoenfeld's woodworking shop.

Mr. Schoenfeld teaches Adam to use a coping saw while the rest of the class watches.

This morning when Mrs. Young gathers her class around her, she asks for volunteers to clean up the painting corner.

The painting corner needs a good coat of background paint to make it ready for displaying artwork.

The children decide to make a mural about things they did during the summer.

One by one the students add their contributions to the mural. Adam's picture is about the trip he made with his family to Disneyland.

Each student does something special to take home at the end of the week. Adam paints a picture of himself.

"Adam, I'm proud of you," his father says. "That's the best self-portrait I've ever seen."

"We're all proud of you," Adam's mother says, and his sister Robbi agrees.

"Me too," says Adam. "School is a pretty good place."